HOLLY KELLER

The Best Present

GREENWILLOW BOOKS
NEW YORK

Watercolor paints and a black pen were
used for the full-color illustrations.
The text type is Zapf Book Medium.

Copyright © 1989 by Holly Keller
from the Publisher, Greenwillow Books,
a division of William Morrow & Company, Inc.,
105 Madison Avenue, New York, N.Y. 10016.
Printed in Singapore by Tien Wah Press
First Edition
1 2 3 4 5 6 7 8 9 10

Library of Congress Cataloging-in-Publication Data
Keller, Holly.
The best present.
Summary: When Rosie is unable to visit
her grandmother in the hospital, she
sends her a special present instead.
[1. Grandmothers—Fiction.
2. Hospitals—Fiction]   I. Title.
PZ7.K28132Bh 1989   [E]   87-38086
ISBN 0-688-07319-0
ISBN 0-688-07320-4 (lib. bdg.)

FOR MY
GRANDMOTHER

Rosie watched Mama get ready to go to the hospital
to see Grandma.

"Why can't I come with you?" she asked.

Mama kissed her on the cheek. "Because you're only
eight, and children under ten are not allowed."

"But Grandma will miss me," Rosie said sadly.

"Yes, she will," Mama said, "but she'll be home in
a week. And I'll be home by lunchtime."

Rosie frowned. "I think it's dumb. I bet
I could make Grandma feel better."
Mama smiled. "I bet you could, too, but
that's the rule."
"How do you know?" Rosie asked.
"Because," Mama said, "there's a big sign in
the lobby that says so."
Mama pressed the tip of Rosie's nose the
way she always did when she was through
talking about something, and picked up
her pocketbook.

Rosie sat on the front steps and watched until Mama went around the corner. It made her stomach ache to think of how Grandma would feel after the operation.

Then she kicked a pebble all the way
down the street to Kate's house.

Rosie looked at herself in Kate's mirror.
"What's the oldest you think I could be?"
she asked Kate.

Kate frowned. "What do you mean?"

"I mean," Rosie said impatiently, "could
I just be eight or could someone think
I was ten?"

Kate scratched her head. "Well, I guess
if you undid your braids and maybe wore
a hat or something, you could be ten."

On Saturday, Rosie put on her new blue sweater and
went to Kate's right after breakfast.
"I'm going to try to visit Grandma," she whispered.
"Will you walk to the hospital with me?"
"Sure," Kate said, "but first we have to dress you up."

She took a hat and some gloves out of the hall closet. Rosie found a purse in Kate's costume box that didn't look too bad. She dropped in the $2.80 she had brought along to buy flowers.

Kate unbraided Rosie's hair and brushed it.

Rosie put on the hat and gloves.

"You look great," Kate said, "and definitely ten."

But Rosie felt a little scared.

Whelan's Flower Shop was on the next street. Rosie jumped when the bell over the door jingled.
"Two dollars and eighty cents will buy you two roses or three carnations," Mr. Whelan said crisply.
Rosie chose the three carnations. Mr. Whelan added some ferns and wrapped everything in green tissue paper.

It was five long blocks to the hospital.

"You better wait here," Rosie whispered to Kate
when they had passed through the automatic
glass doors.

"How will you know where to go?" Kate whispered
back. Rosie shrugged. "I know she's on the seventh
floor because Mama said. I guess I'll just take
the elevator up."

Rosie adjusted her hat and started walking.
The corridor seemed to go on forever.

There were some signs on the wall near the elevators. One of them was that rule about ten-year-olds. A man in a green uniform was standing near the signs. He told people where to go and answered their questions.
He eyed Rosie carefully.
"Excuse me, young lady," he said finally as she edged toward the elevator door, "children under ten are not allowed upstairs."
Rosie swallowed hard. She opened her mouth to speak, but nothing came out. "I am ten," she wanted to say, but she couldn't. She could feel everyone's eyes on her, and her own were filling up with tears.

Rosie held up the flowers.
"Could you give these to my Grandma Alice on
the seventh floor?"
"Going up," the elevator man called as he took
the flowers, and the elevator door slammed shut.

Rosie made Kate promise not to tell anyone what had happened. She tried not to even think about Grandma and the stupid flowers. When she had to pass Mr. Whelan's store, she crossed over to the other side of the street.

When Grandma finally came home, Mama
took Rosie to visit her after school. Grandma
was resting in the big armchair.
Rosie went over to give her a kiss.

"What's in the box?" Rosie asked.

"Sit down with me and I'll show you," Grandma said.

Rosie squeezed in next to her, and Grandma took
out all the get-well cards people had sent her.

"They're pretty," Rosie said.

Her throat felt a little strange.

"I got some presents, too," Grandma said. "Aunt Edith
   sent me lilac scented bath powder, and Uncle Henry
   sent me this nice book."
Grandma opened it to a page that was marked, and
   there were Rosie's three carnations neatly pressed
   in the green tissue paper.
"But this," Grandma said softly, "was the best present
   of all."

"How come you didn't tell anybody you got them?" Rosie asked.

Grandma smiled. "I just had a feeling it was a secret."

Rosie stared at the pattern in the rug. "They wouldn't let me up in the elevator," she said.

"I know," Grandma said, "but it was very brave of you to try."

"I missed you," Rosie said, trying not to cry.

"I missed you, too," Grandma said, "and the flowers made me feel better than all the visitors."

"Really?" Rosie asked.

"Really," Grandma said.

Rosie gave Grandma a hug, wiped her eyes, and
wriggled off the chair. Then she went to help Mama
bring some tea and cookies into the living room.
The cookies were the good kind from the bakery,
and they smelled wonderful.